This dragon book belongs to:

....

A Dragon With ADHD
My Dragon Books - Volume 41
Written by Steve Herman

ISBN: 978-1-64916-095-9 (paperback)
ISBN: 978-1-64916-096-6 (hardcover)

www.MyDragonBooks.com

First Edition: March 2021
10 9 8 7 6 5 4 3 2 1

A Dragon With ADHD

My Dragon Books - Volume 41

Steve Herman

The most important thing
that Diggory had to figure out
Was to keep from getting mad
and blowing fire right out his snout.

If you pay close attention,
I am pretty sure you'll see
That the lessons Diggory's learned
can help kids like you and me.

Take for instance, this one time when Diggory was upset, But he learned something about himself he'd never forget!

Diggory Doo was full of energy and couldn't stay in his chair;

If you tell Diggory Doo to GO, he's already there!

But when he was in the classroom, where he was supposed to sit, That was not what Diggory wanted to do – not one little bit.

Diggory's teacher fussed at him
because he talked a lot –
He interrupted when she was teaching,
even though he knew he should NOT.

Diggory tried to stop, but no matter how he tried,

WOOOOOOW!!!

His words came spilling out –
They would not stay inside!

Excessive talking seemed to be
what Diggory most enjoyed,
And sometimes when he was talking,
he couldn't control his voice;

He got a bit excited,
and whatever he was telling

Gets louder by the minute
until Diggory Doo was yelling!

Diggory played with building blocks –
He stacked them way up tall,
But before he was even finished,
he grabbed his basketball...

He got all his crayons out
and prepared to draw a while,
But stopped to work on a puzzle –
It seemed it was his style.

He never quite finished
any task that he's begun –
He quit and moved to something else
long before he's done.

He took toys out to play,
but couldn't remember where he left them,
So then he had to search
when he wanted to go and get them.

"When you have extra energy, Diggory,
you could run –
Just choose a proper time and place!
Wouldn't that be fun?"

"You have imagination –
I love the stories that you tell.
You're my favorite friend to play with.
You're smart and kind, as well."

"I wouldn't change you, Diggory Doo –
You're a shining star –
ADHD is what you have –
It isn't what you are!"